Suddenly, life in Horseshoe Bend seems exciting.
For some unknown reason, Cousin Sophy and her
daughter Lilybell have come to town. And they've
brought along the biggest trunk Susie Conroy has
ever seen.

Susie has made up her mind to find out what's
hiding in the trunk. Watch what happens when
Susie solves

The Giant Trunk Mystery

Winner Books are produced by Victor Books and are designed to entertain and instruct young readers in Christian principles. Each book has been approved by specialists in Christian education and children's literature. These books uphold the teachings and principles of the Bible.

Other Winner Books you will enjoy:

Sarah and the Magic Twenty-fifth, by Margaret Epp
Sarah and the Pelican, by Margaret Epp
Sarah and the Lost Friendship, by Margaret Epp
Sarah and the Mystery of the Hidden Boy, by Margaret Epp
Sarah and the Darnley Boys, by Margaret Epp
The Hairy Brown Angel and Other Animal Tails, edited by Grace Fox Anderson
The Peanut Butter Hamster and Other Animal Tails, edited by Grace Fox Anderson
Danger on the Alaskan Trail (three mysteries)
Gopher Hole Treasure Hunt, by Ralph Bartholomew
Daddy, Come Home, by Irene Aiken
Battle at the Blue Line, by P. C. Fredricks
Patches, by Edith Buck
The Taming of Cheetah, by Lee Roddy
Ted and the Secret Club, by Bernard Palmer
The Mystery Man of Horseshoe Bend, by Linda Boorman
Colby Moves West, by Sharon Miller

Mother of three, a children's worker in her church, and a former public school teacher, LINDA BOORMAN has shared stories with children for 20 years. Now she is writing her own, and her unusual sense of humor makes her stories delightful.

Mrs. Boorman lives in Frenchtown, Montana. She is a graduate of Multnomah School of the Bible and received her B.S. in Education from Eastern Oregon State College. Her earlier years were spent near small Oregon towns similar to the fictitious Horseshoe Bend of this novel, her second book.

The Giant Trunk Mystery

by Linda Boorman

illustrated by
Marilee Harrald

A WINNER BOOK

VICTOR BOOKS
a division of SP Publications, Inc.
WHEATON. ILLINOIS 60187

Offices also in Fullerton, California • Whitby, Ontario, Canada • Amersham-on-the-Hill, Bucks, England

All Scripture quotations are from the King James Version.

Library of Congress Catalog Card Number: 80-54121
ISBN: 0-88207-491-1

VICTOR BOOKS
A division of SP Publications, Inc.
P.O. Box 1825, Wheaton, Ill. 60187

Contents

1 The Trunk Arrives   9

2 Something Goes Thump   20

3 A Discovery   29

4 The "Wanted" Poster   39

5 Problems with a Periscope   47

6 A Wrong Guess   54

7 A Ruined Chance   61

8 Look-Alikes   67

9 What the Trunk Held   73

10 Putting Things to Rights   86

Life in 1898   90

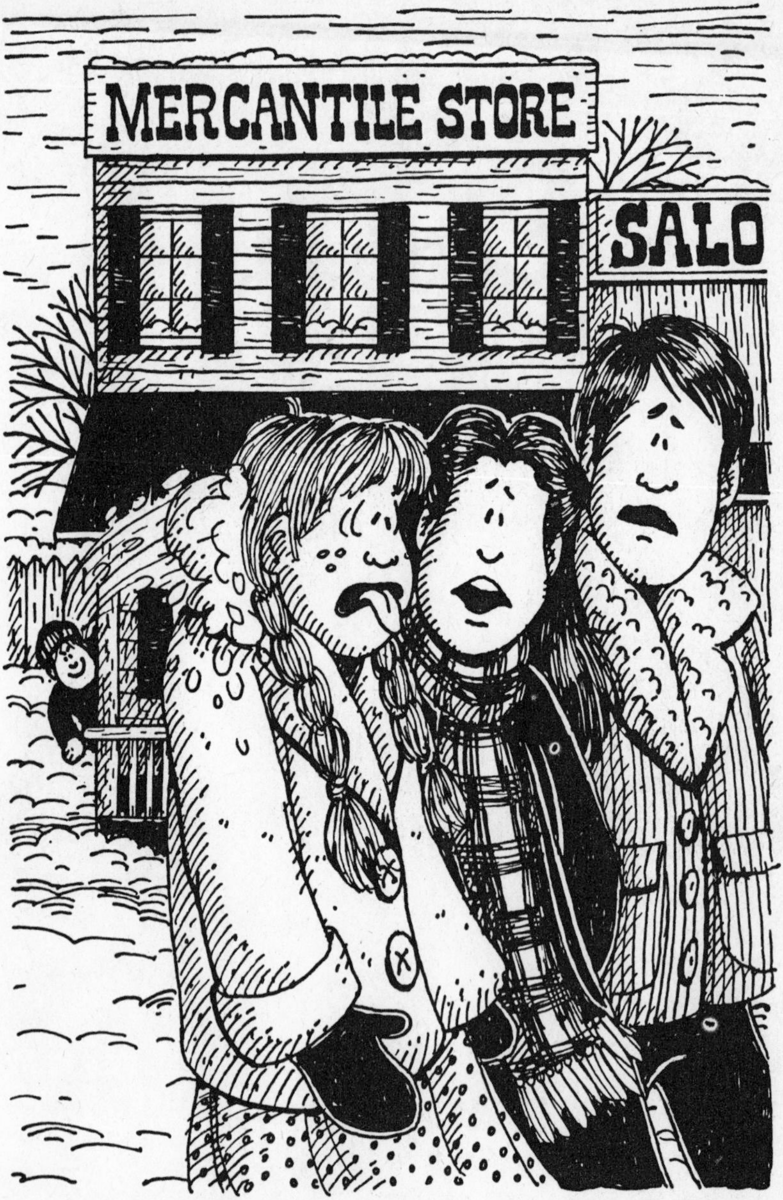
MERCANTILE STORE
SALO

1
The Trunk Arrives

Most of the citizens of Horseshoe Bend* will think back on the winter of 1898 as the terrible winter of the influenza* outbreak. I remember it as the winter I discovered love*, and the contents of Cousin Sophy's trunk.

The sickness did affect me. But not by knocking me flat on my back in bed. It got to me by way of my family.

Papa, being the preacher of the Horseshoe Bend Bible Church, was kept on the move day and night.

You can find an explanation of the starred words under Life in 1898 on pages 90-94.

People wanted a preacher to pray with them when the influenza had them in its grip. And they especially needed Papa's comfort when they had to say "good-bye" to someone who didn't recover.

That horrid sickness didn't bypass the parsonage, either. My next oldest sister, Abby, and our baby brother, Timmy, were laid low.

Mama, who could cool a feverish forehead with a touch of her hand, scurried between their beds.

Aunt Minnie, Papa's sister who lived with us, stirred up tasty soups to tempt their appetites.

After Cousin Sophy came to town, the sickness grabbed my 12-year-old twin, Tommy, and my ornery 6-year-old brother, Joe.

That left me, Susie Conroy, and my oldest sister, Sarah, still on two feet. And it's a good thing I was as healthy as a weed or I might never have solved the mystery of the giant trunk.

I first laid eyes on that trunk after school, a week before Valentine's Day.

Miss Prim had stood behind her desk, clapping her hands for attention. "Boys and girls, it's time for dismissal. Due to the influenza epidemic keeping so many of our pupils home, we only have a few valentine poems to submit to *The Chronicle*. But, I believe it's important that we do so. People need to feed their minds on something besides thieves and sickness. So, Susie Conroy and Agnes Miller, will you drop these poems off at the newspaper office on your way home?"

I glanced over at Agnes Miller (known as "Sis" to her friends) and grinned. We silently agreed that we'd be delighted to do that errand.

Mr. Evans, the owner of the newspaper, had objected to printing our literary efforts at the beginning. He, also being the sheriff, leaned more toward legal news.

Miss Prim had persisted. She'd been our teacher only one term, but we'd already discovered that her soft exterior covered a hard core.

Mr. Smith, our previous teacher, had caught gold fever and headed off to try his luck at mining. Gold mining was a big thing in the hills and canyons of eastern Oregon in 1898. Although Horseshoe Bend country was high desert and ran more to ranching, the mines were close enough that news often filtered in from the gold camps. So far we'd heard no news of Mr. Smith striking it rich. But, he'd said he'd rather starve searching for gold in the ground then for wisdom in our heads.

While I rearranged the mess in my desk, I watched Jake Evans out of the corner of my eye. I caught my breath and dared to hope that he might walk to the newspaper office with us.

He kind of hung around the door, while we collected the poems from Miss Prim's desk. Then I had to tell Tommy that I'd be going to the hotel to see if Mrs. Higgins needed me. My sister, Abby, generally worked at the Grande Hotel, but I was helping do her job while she was sick.

Tommy was standing on the upended woodbox trying to fasten a wire around the drooping stovepipe. Miss Prim held the box steady and told him he should be on the school board. Tommy is always thinking of things to fix. I'm the one that's usually in a fix.

Jake carried in some wood, while Sis and I wrapped and pulled on our outside clothes. Just as we got to the door, Jake pulled it open for us and we met a chilly blast of wind together.

He gave us his good-natured grin as he fell in step beside me. "Pa's working on a good case right now," he told us as we followed the dirty path of snow across the school yard toward the row of false-fronted buildings. "He's hot on the trail of some guy who's been selling salted mining* stock."

"Salted mining stock! What's that?" I squeaked, forgetting my resolve to speak in a moderate voice.

"It's where they stick enough gold in a no-good mine to make it look like it's loaded. Then, they sell stocks or shares, saying it's a producing gold mine."

Sis was in the middle of asking Jake how anyone could be so stupid, when I felt the sting of a snowball on the back of my head.

I whirled around in time to see Joe dodge out of sight behind the mercantile store*. A second later, he poked his head out and yelled, "Susie's in love with Jake. It's enough to give you a bellyache."

Sis and Jake turned around when they heard all the screeching. I had a violent urge to pound Joe into the ground, but I knew young ladies trying to impress young men couldn't afford to resort to such coarse behavior.

So I did what was next best. I pointedly ignored him and marched on as though I hadn't heard a word. My companions did the same. But I knew by the smirk on Sis' face and the questioning look Jake gave me that they'd heard.

I was sure my face was as red as my hair and I knew my Irish* temper was at its boiling point. Only our arrival at the newspaper office saved me from disgracing myself and hotfooting off after Joe.

I dashed through the door, just as Joe and another little hooligan from school ran up behind me and screamed, "Susie's in love with Jake—" The door slamming behind Jake cut off the rest of that embarrassing jingle.

As our eyes adjusted to the dim interior, we discovered Jake's father sitting behind his desk, with his chair tipped back and his feet on the desk top. Today he seemed to be busy doing the sheriff's part of his work.

Behind the desk was a large caged-off corner where the prisoners were kept. As usual the jail was empty. Only once in a while, Dirty Duffy from the Lightning Rod Saloon had to be locked up for disturbing the peace. Then Jake's mother, who was a strong temperance advocate (meaning she pressed hard for getting rid of all alcoholic drinks) would practice her speech on him.

The other side of the room held the black, inky-smelling printing press where Jake and his father ran off *The Chronicle* once a week.

Any other time I would have lingered, but Joe had spoiled the joy of being escorted by the school's most handsome boy. I felt a strong urge to escape from the "object of my affections."

I slapped the poems down on Sheriff Evans' desk and yanked Sis out the door with me, before he could get his feet off the desk.

"Oh, Sis, how horrible!" I wailed the minute the door closed. "How could that Joe! Just wait until I get my hands on him. The first time Jake makes a point of walking with me and—"

Sis grabbed my coat sleeve and looking me right

in the eye, said, "Susie, I think he may be smitten with you. Oh, he's so tall and dark and handsome. It's so romantic. Aren't you excited?" she asked as she twirled around.

"Stop jumping around, Sis, and tell me something. Remember, friends don't lie. Do you see anything about me that he could possibly like?"

"Well, yes, you're friendly and, well, lots of men like red hair and—"

"Oh, Sis, I do wish I had blond curls. Or at least a peaches-and-cream complexion or raven-black hair like Mama and Sarah. Why'd *I* have to inherit the Conroy look? Red hair, freckles, bones that stick out everywhere—"

Sis interrupted my complaining with, "Susie, look! They've put a valentine display in the drugstore window."

We'd walked from the newspaper office to the drugstore without my even being aware of it. The possibilities of having an admirer swept ordinary events, like walking, out of my head.

"Susie, look at that box of candy," Sis continued, "the huge heart-shaped one with the satin pillow top and bow. Isn't it a beauty? I'll bet it would cost a gold nugget."

"Yeah, no one we know could afford it," I said, as I pictured a tall, dark, 14-year-old presenting that box to a redheaded, 12-going-on-13-year-old.

After the mist cleared from my brain, I saw my sister, Sarah, and her husband-to-be, Sidney Wright, waving at us from behind the drugstore display. They planned to be married a week from Saturday and set up housekeeping in the rooms over the drugstore, since Sidney and his father owned the store. Being in love had transformed them from people who were barely tolerable to a first-rate couple.

Waving good-bye to them, we set off at a run toward the hotel. Suddenly, I stopped Sis. A new thought, one so important that it had to be expressed, popped into my head.

"Sis, do you suppose love is contagious? In the air, I mean. Doc says this influenza that's going around is in the air. So, why couldn't love be like that? With all the to-do about Sarah's wedding and valentine love and all, I think I'm catching it!"

"Could be," Sis agreed. "Guess I'd better stay away from you or I might catch it too."

We walked the rest of the way to the Grande Hotel in silence, our breath making a fog in the cold air, as our feet crunched in the frozen snow. *This weather isn't helping the influenza cases*, I thought grimly.

I parted with Sis under the sagging hotel sign.

Sis' grandparents lived just beyond the hotel. She stayed with them during the school week, since her father's ranch was so far from town.

Skipping up the steps, I let myself into the dusky hotel hall and nearly collided with a huge, bulky object.

Inspecting it in the fast-fading light, I discovered the object was the biggest trunk I'd ever seen. As I rubbed my hands over the scratchy horsehide covering, Mrs. Higgins waddled into the hall.

"Land-to-goodness, am I glad to see you, Susie." She stopped, folded her hands across her front, and glared at the trunk. "If this hasn't been an afternoon to make a widow woman wish she'd taken in washing instead of house guests. See that thing?" she asked, as she pointed a pudgy finger toward the trunk.

"I almost ran into it."

"Well, that belongs to Mrs. High-and-Mighty and her dainty daughter. She comes hoity-toitying in here making all sorts of demands. The man that brung her into town positively refused to carry the thing upstairs. Took all the strength him and Mac MacDonald could muster to get it in the hall."

"What's in it?"

"How'd I know? They said it felt like a load of horseshoes, but she don't say. Just says it's got to be put into her room immediately," Mrs. Higgins answered, all her loose flesh shaking with indignation.

"What do you want me to do tonight?" I asked, changing the subject.

"There's plenty, believe you me," Mrs. Higgins told me, as she mumbled on about her troubles. "Mrs. Sophy Stoddard, that's her name, and her daughter insisted on an upstairs front room that opened outside. Now you know I couldn't give them a front room. Sheriff Evans and his family's had the front ones on one side for years and I expect Grandpa Murdock'll die in his on the other side. She said they *must* at least have an outside door. So, I gave them the room at the end of the hall to the right. It has that door that opens to them steps that go up the outside of the building."

Barely listening to her ramblings, I polished the trunk's brass fittings with my finger. "It sure looks new and costly with all this brass."

"Oh, I 'spects she's got money, cause she wants her food sent up and said she'll pay for it. Probably figures she's too good to eat with the other boarders."

"How're you going to get her trunk upstairs?"

"Your pa's coming over, soon as he can. Oh, I shouldn't be speaking ill of them. They're some kind of kin of your ma's."

"Of Mama's?" I squeaked in amazement.

"Third cousin twice removed, or something like that. Believe you me, they don't act nothing like your sweet little ma. They even came to town planning to stay at you folks', but with Abby and the baby sick, that was out of the question. Mrs. Stoddard seemed plum put out that she had to stay in a public house. Your ma and Aunt Minnie don't need no more work put on them, with all that sickness and a wedding coming up."

"I sure never heard of any relatives of Mama's by that name, but at least, now I'll find out what's in this big trunk," I muttered to myself.

"Land-to-goodness, here we stand flapping our jaws, with dinner to get on the table. Susie, you get the table set. Other people will be eating at it, even if Mrs. High-and-Mighty thinks it's beneath her."

My curiosity nearly had the best of me. As I followed Mrs. Higgins' broad back into the dining room, I wondered if these relatives were as bad as Mrs. Higgins made them out to be. And the trunk— I could hardly wait to find out why they were traveling with such an enormous trunk.

2
Something Goes Thump

The plates were set on the table and I'd just picked up the dishpan of silverware, when I first laid eyes on my cousins. I nearly dropped the pan. Mrs. Higgins' description of my distant kin hadn't prepared me for such charmers.

They sailed into the dining room looking for all the world like a queen and a princess. Instead of making her look drab, the mother's widow's clothes* played up her fragile beauty.

I only caught a glimpse of the daughter standing behind her mother, but she seemed some sort of heavenly vision.

"Girl, where's that Mrs. Higgins?" my cousin demanded in a voice like lemonade with ice and no sugar.

Her beauty crumbled, as she carried on, "Well, where is she? That trunk must be moved to my room. I've never seen such a shabby establishment."

"She's in the kitchen," I told her as I plopped the dishpan on the table. "I'll go get her."

"Well, I should hope so. The service around here—" she exclaimed, as she flounced around and sailed into Papa.

"Sure and what have we here?" Papa asked as he pushed her away.

She stopped her griping long enough to take note of Papa's height. Then exchanging her huffy look for a totally helpless one, she asked him, "Sir, would you be kind enough to help a poor widow with her trunk?"

"Sure and 'twas for that very reason I stepped over here. My wife informed me of your need. As soon as ever I wept with the Carlsons over the going home of their little fellow, I came."

"Not little Johnny!" I cried out, as I remembered his little blond head popping over the church pew in front of me.

Papa grabbed my hand and gave it a little squeeze. " 'Twas best for him, he's with Jesus now.

'Tis his mama and papa that'll be needing our comfort, Susie."

We were reminded of my cousins again, when Cousin Sophy cleared her throat.

Papa extended his big hand and said, "Sure and I'm Neil Conroy, better known as Brother Conroy, a preacher of the Gospel. And 'twould seem you're Cousin Sophy Stoddard, kin to my little lass of a wife."

"Pleased to meet you," Cousin Sophy replied in a honey-sweet voice. "And this," she told us as she pushed her forward, "is my 13-year-old daughter, Lilybell."

Lilybell, that beautiful vision in a ruffle-trimmed dress, blinked her huge blue eyes and whispered, "How do you do?" Her blond curls bobbed as she did a slight curtsy.

Papa introduced me as his lovely, youngest daughter. In his eyes I wasn't a scrawny stick in an ink-spattered school dress.

The introductions were no more than finished when Jake came banging in the hotel door, stomping the snow from his feet.

"Good evening, Brother Conroy," he called as he saw Papa standing in the doorway between the hall and dining room.

"Sure and aren't you just the lad I'm needing.

Come and give me a hand with that giant-sized trunk sitting there in the hall."

Cousin Sophy swung into action. "Now, Cousin Neil, that trunk must be handled very carefully. It *must* not be dropped, jarred, nor can it be tipped too much. . . ."

Papa grabbed one of the handholds, while Jake caught hold of the other. Papa's no weakling and Jake's big and strong for a 14-year-old, but they could barely lift it off the floor.

"Sure and what be in this thing?" Papa gasped, as he caught his breath.

"Now, Cousin Neil, it's not polite to ask a lady about the contents of her trunk," Cousin Sophy told him teasingly.

"Sure and for all the world, it feels like a load of bricks," Papa said as he turned to Jake. " 'Twould seem best to push it to the staircase, then find a plank to scoot it up the stairs."

Papa might just as well have been talking to the wall—Jake had discovered Lilybell. He stood there looking all pop-eyed, as she peered from under those long lashes and cooed, "Ooh, you're so strong."

Jake did come out of his trance long enough to hunt up a long board. Then, while Papa pulled, he and I pushed that ponderous trunk up those stairs.

Cousin Sophy cautioned us to be careful every time we moved, while Lilybell oohed and aahed about Jake's great strength.

It's a wonder Jake didn't carry it up alone. He certainly put on enough of a show. No one mentioned the fact that I popped a button and split a seam assisting.

When we finally reached the top, Mrs. Higgins showed up and told me to get back to the dining room. "There are *other* boarders that need feeding," she stated, as she gave Cousin Sophy a hard look.

So I was forced back to my duties, leaving Jake in the clutches of Lilybell and never getting a chance for one peek into the trunk.

"And it was only this afternoon that Jake's escorting me from school made me as happy as a sunflower in May," I muttered as I tossed the silverware around.

Outside of one episode, the evening went along like most in the hotel. All the boarders ate and settled down to their usual winter evening activities. But instead of playing checkers with Grandpa Murdock, like he normally did, Jake took off upstairs.

Then, Cousin Sophy and Mrs. Higgins had another set-to. Cousin Sophy complained that the lock on her door didn't work and Mrs. Higgins said she always kept trustworthy boarders, so Cousin Sophy didn't need a lock.

Cousin Sophy looked mad enough to chew nails. She said she'd use the back of a chair. But Mrs. Higgins got in the last word by saying that only the untrustworthy didn't trust other people.

By the time I'd finished my chores, I was exhausted. It had been a long up-and-down sort of day and God seemed far away.

I was just getting my coat from the hook in the hall when Mama and Aunt Minnie came in the door. I was so glad to see their cheerful faces that I squealed, "Did you come to walk me home?"

"Sure and 'tis the way home you could be finding, Susie," Aunt Minnie declared as she shook the snow from her and produced a plate covered with a tea towel from under her coat. "Your mama and I figured we'd deliver some of my spice cookies to her Cousin Sophy. Did you meet her yourself, Susie?"

"Yes, but Mama, I never knew you had a Cousin Sophy."

Mama answered, "If the truth be known, neither did I, Susie. From what she told me, she's a daughter of a cousin of mine from back East. Seems he told her about my living in Horseshoe Bend before she came out here. She's rather vague about when she lost her husband and all—"

"Sure and wasn't there something to do with a trunk?" Aunt Minnie asked, her curiosity matching my own.

"Yes."

"Minnie, I believe Susie must be worn out, she's being so quiet!" Mama exclaimed, as she felt my forehead. "With all this influenza, we'd best get her home."

As dear as Mama is, I couldn't explain to her that my drooping spirits were caused by a case of love-sickness teamed up with a broken heart.

"Sure and 'tis best we be getting these delivered. And would you be knowing what room's hers, Susie?"

As I led them up the stairs to the far room at the right, the aroma from Aunt Minnie's spice cookies seemed to push the stale air from the hall.

Aunt Minnie's loud knock echoed through the long hall.

"Ooh, is that you, Jakey?" Lilybell murmured as she opened the door a crack and peered into the hall.

"LILYBELL STODDARD, *SHUT* THAT DOOR!" Cousin Sophy shrieked.

Aunt Minnie, who's big like Papa, stuck her foot in the door and pushed it open wide.

Through the open door, I saw Cousin Sophy fling

the trunk lid shut. Just after it closed, something inside thumped. Then the trunk jiggled and shuffled and fell silent.

Cousin Sophy quickly turned around and put on her "pleased to meet you" face.

"Sure and 'twas a little something to nibble on we brung you," Aunt Minnie said, as she handed over the plate.

"My, how sweet of you."

"Yes, and to see if there's anything you need," Mama added. "We're so sorry that we couldn't open our home to you, but with two members of the family abed with influenza, it didn't seem wise."

"Please don't let it bother you. We're very comfortable here," Cousin Sophy assured us as she practically pushed us out the door.

"Sure and she's an odd stick," Aunt Minnie commented as the door slammed behind us.

"She does seem to lack God's peace. We must pray and see what we can do to help," Mama told us as we left the hotel.

Unfortunately, I was too busy speculating about the trunk to heed what Mama said. *Why was Cousin Sophy so secretive about her trunk? What could it have in it that needed to be handled so carefully? And whatever would a lady carry in her trunk that went thump, thump?*

3
A Discovery

"I tell you there's something mysterious about that trunk," I told my brother Tommy on our way to school the next morning.

"Just because it's big doesn't make it mysterious," Tommy objected. "Lots of ladies travel with big trunks. And they're fussy about them too."

"Maybe so, but they're not so heavy a man can't pick them up. And they don't wiggle and thump after the lids are slammed shut," I reminded him as we arrived at the foot of the hotel steps.

Mama had suggested we go by the hotel and see if Lilybell wanted to go to school. She being new and all, Mama said that was the kind thing to do.

"Say, Tommy let's go around to the side and go up those outside steps. Their room has a door that opens onto them. We'll knock and see if they invite us in. Then you'll see what I mean when I say that trunk is the biggest in the country."

Just as we got around the corner by the steps, Tommy stopped me. "Look there's footprints in the snow. Someone with big feet has been down those steps and back up since it quit snowing this morning. Does Cousin Sophy or Lilybell have big feet?"

"They're about as big as a fleabite," I answered bitterly.

"Hmmmm." Tommy screwed up his freckled nose and looked up and down the steps. "Susie, did you notice that transom?"

"That what-some?"

"That little hinged window over the door to their room. If there was only some way we could see in it. Hmmm, I bet a periscope*, like I read about in the *Scientific American* magazine, would work."

I hadn't the foggiest notion of what Tommy was mumbling about, but he's a thinker and inventor, so I felt sure we'd soon know all there was to know about that trunk.

Before we had time to start up the stairs, the hotel door opened. Lilybell tripped out with Jake.

They made a striking couple. He looked so manly with dainty Lilybell hanging on his arm, squealing, "Oh, Jakey, don't let me fall on the ice. Ooh, you've such a strong arm to cling to."

My dreams of being Jake's girl nearly vanished then and there. How could I compete with this blue-eyed charmer wrapped up in a sky-blue cape with enough braid trim on it to rope a calf?

However, I seemed to be the only one, outside of Miss Prim, who thought Lilybell was a pain.

Lilybell was no more than enrolled in school and she'd captivated the whole class with her "sweet" helpless manner. Even Tommy and Sis couldn't understand my nasty attitude.

Miss Prim appeared to be annoyed with all the evasive giggling and eye-batting she got when she questioned Lilybell about her background. Lilybell seemed to be a dunce in every subject but penmanship. That was, till afternoon recess.

She came back from the hotel with the most elegant valentine poem ever. (She also made it back without "Jakey's" arm, since he'd stayed at school to take part in a snowball war.)

After informing Miss Prim that she'd written a valentine poem, Lilybell was allowed to read it to the school. With her eyes glued on Jake, she began, "Can hearts in which true love is plighted . . ."

and continued in this manner for some 25 verses.

When she finished, everyone but Miss Prim and I applauded. After all, the rest of us had been hard-pressed to write 10 lines for our valentine poems.

Miss Prim, with one eyebrow raised, merely questioned, "You did this yourself?"

About then, Sis, who'd been acting rather lifeless all day, had to leave school. Miss Prim sent Jake for Sis' grandfather who helped her home. She'd caught the influenza sickness, instead of lovesickness.

The cloudy sky was low and threatening when I dashed into the hotel after school. After finding out Mrs. Higgins didn't need me, I hurried toward the door, hoping to make it out before Lilybell showed up with "Jakey."

Jake's mother caught me just as I reached the door. "Susie, would you please give your mother a message?"

"Sure."

"Tell her that we're having an organizational meeting of the Horseshoe Bend Temperance Society* tomorrow afternoon in the hotel lobby. We especially want her to come and your father too if he can. It always looks good to have the preacher offer prayer."

"I'll tell her."

"Don't forget now," she called after me, as the

door swung shut with a loud bang.

But I nearly did. It wasn't until the seven of us (Timmy and Abby were still in bed) had polished off the last of Aunt Minnie's Irish stew that I remembered.

We'd all settled back in our chairs around our big kitchen table, feeling cozy and content. The wind was howling up another storm and throwing bits of frozen snow against the windowpanes. But inside, our big cookstove purred and the kerosene lamp* cast a warm glow across the red-checked tablecloth. Lying under the table, Old Sniffer, our dog, made a first-rate footstool and I'd nearly dozed off, when Papa cleared his throat.

"Sure and I wouldn't have known, but Sheriff Evans is having quite a piece in today's *Chronicle* to do with mine salting."

" 'Tis past understanding why a body'd be taken in," Aunt Minnie commented as she spooned up the bread pudding.

"And I'll be telling you, 'tis wanting to get rich prompt-like 'twill make people believe those lies. 'Twould seem though that Sheriff Evans, in cahoots with some government men, is hot on the trail of one of the crooks. Sure and I wouldn't have known, but he sneaked out of Dry Gulch right under the noses of the lawmen."

I jerked up, when Papa, abruptly changing the subject, looked at me and said, "Well now, Susie, bless me, but 'twould seem your name be in the news, also."

"It—it is?" I stammered.

"Sure and something to do with hearts and flowers."

"Oh, that's our valentine poems we're doing at school. Miss Prim is having Mr. Evans print them," I explained as I felt my cheeks getting warm.

"Sure and what blather. 'Tis wasting your time, you be," Aunt Minnie sniffed.

"Well now, appears to me God's got considerable to say about love. Hand me my Bible, Becka, off'n the sideboard," Papa told Mama, "and we'll be having a look at a chapter that God wrote on that very topic."

While Mama bent toward the sideboard, the light shining on her black hair reminded me of Mrs. Evans' message.

"Mama, I nearly forgot. Mrs. Evans wants you and Papa to come to a meeting tomorrow at the hotel. She's organizing a Horseshoe Bend Temperance Society."

"Oh," Mama answered and looked at Papa.

"Sure and you know my thinkings to do with that," Papa boomed out in his best preaching voice.

" 'Twill not cure any man a whit by taking his bottle from him. 'Tis the heart that's sinful, so God says, and 'tis the heart that needs changing. Sure and when God's invited in, the heart is changed and there'll be new longings. Drinking alcohol 'twill not be one of them."

"But," Papa continued in a softer voice, " 'tis my notion you'd best go. I'm for thinking you'll be having a calming influence on that hen party. As for me, I'll stay to home."

"I do believe, *party* is the right word," Mama said as she tucked a strand of hair into its bun. "With all this sickness and grief and bitter weather, I believe the ladies are anxious for just a bit of social time together."

"And I'm for thinking you'd best go," Aunt Minnie agreed. "Sure and you'll be ruining your eyesight with all that sewing on the wedding clothes. It'll not be hurting me one bit to be doing some of it for you."

Papa echoed Aunt Minnie. "Well now, I'll be playing nurse. It's a bit of lady chitchat you be needing."

I listened to my elders in amazement. Here Aunt Minnie and Papa seemed to be gladly offering themselves so Mama could spend an afternoon of pleasant visiting. And everyone in Horseshoe Bend and the surrounding countryside knew how Aunt Minnie loathed sewing and Papa detested nursing sick people.

I should have understood, after Papa turned to 1 Corinthians 13 and read, "Charity . . . seeketh not her own."

And, "Charity . . . is not easily provoked," should have explained why Mama said what she did, even after Cousin Sophy had been so snippy to her the evening before.

Mama said, "Susie, you stop tomorrow morning on your way to school and invite Cousin Sophy to the temperance meeting. Mrs. Evans might overlook inviting her. I still don't understand why Sophy's here in town, she doesn't say, but she must get terribly lonely sitting in that hotel room."

I convinced Mama that I'd have more time right then. So, while they were clearing up after supper, I scooted over to the hotel.

Because Tommy had a cough, Mama wouldn't let him accompany me. I did want him to see the size of that trunk.

No one seemed to be about as I let myself into the hotel hall. Then, I heard a titter from the dining room, and, "Oh, Jakey, you're just too-too clever. Now, how'd you say you worked the next sum*?"

I scurried up the steps.

I waited outside Cousin Sophy's door several minutes after knocking. A cold draft of air blew from under it. I wondered if Cousin Sophy had just gone out the other door, letting in the cold air.

But she finally opened the door, and invited me into her room.

"Yes?" she inquired.

"Mama sent me over to invite—to invite—" I stammered to a halt. There on the top of that huge trunk sat a half-full whiskey bottle with an empty one lying on its side. Cousin Sophy quickly stepped between the trunk and me.

I sputtered out the rest of my message and scuttled down the hall.

As unlikely as it seemed, I may have discovered the contents of Cousin Sophy's trunk! Could it be full of whiskey bottles?

As I crept down the stairs, I heard Lilybell's shrill little voice demand, "Now show me again how you did that sum, Jakey."

The bitter cold outside revived my brain. Wouldn't "Jakey," whose mother was so strong on temperance, be interested in knowing that darling Lilybell's mother kept a trunk load of whiskey in their room? Now, how could I prove it?

4
"The "Wanted" Poster"

"I must have imagined something in that trunk wiggling," I told Tommy as we set out for school the morning after the "great discovery."

"Really."

"Yes." Leaning close to him, I whispered excitedly, "It's full of whiskey bottles. She must have come to town to sell illegal whiskey."

"You mean a bootlegger*?"

"Yeah!"

"Did you see the bottles inside the trunk?"

"No, but they must be in there. There were two bottles on the top and they explain a lot of things:

39

why the trunk was so heavy and needed to be handled so carefully and why those man-sized footprints were on the steps yesterday morning. They must have been a customer's."

"Aw, Susie, you can't be sure of that." Tommy didn't try to hide the fact that he didn't believe me.

"That's the trouble. But I mean to find out. A lot depends on it."

"The periscope ought to help. I've figured out how to make one. As soon as I can get a couple of mirrors, I can put it together. I'm borrowing the pipe out of the sink. Aunt Minnie doesn't use it in the winter anyway."

"Just what's a periscope and how's that going to help us get a look inside that trunk?"

"I read about one in the *Scientific American* magazine and thought it might come in handy someday. Sure enough, this is just what we need. We can stand outside their door after dark and look right into their room."

"Without opening the door?"

"Sure, you take a pipe and put a bend in each end; ours already has the bends, I checked under the house yesterday after school. Then you stick a mirror in the crook of each bend. Put the top of the pipe to the window over the door and look into the mirror at the other end and it shows you the mirror at the top end which reflects what's going on right in their room."

It sounded rather involved to me, but I had great faith in Tommy's abilities. It was all so exciting we hardly noticed Joe pelting us with snowballs all the way to the schoolhouse.

By the time we'd arrived at the school yard, we'd planned to borrow the mirrors from Sarah. (Since love had hit her, she'd become extremely generous.)

Tommy would spend Saturday constructing this marvelous invention.

"We might not need it, though," I told Tommy. "I figure I might be able to get into their room after school tonight. I'll go straight to the hotel and Cousin Sophy should be at the temperance meeting. No doubt Lilybell will be batting her eyes at Jake," I added grimly, "so, their room will be empty."

"The trunk might be locked."

"I'll try, anyway."

I never had a chance to even try. Mrs. Higgins grabbed me the minute I came in the door. She needed me to pass refreshments to the ladies at the temperance meeting.

While I passed the cake around, Mrs. Evans handed out printed copies of "Ten Nights in a Barroom and What I Saw There." I never had time to find out what the writer saw in a barroom and judging by the chatter, neither did the ladies. The talk ran more toward whether skirts were going to be fuller this year and how Mrs. Miller got the liver spots off her hands, than what went on in a bar-room.

Since I noticed Cousin Sophy at the meeting, I hotfooted it for the stairs as soon as my tray was empty.

But I met Mrs. Higgins waddling down the steps before I had time to get up them. She told me two lawmen had just registered.

"So, land-to-goodness, we've got to get supper on the table." She acted as though they'd arrest her if she didn't feed them on time, and insisted she needed my help promptly.

I couldn't very well tell her that I needed the time to break into my cousin's room, so I followed her out to the kitchen, thankful that Tommy knew about such things as periscopes.

After the hustle and bustle of getting dinner on the table, Mrs. Higgins heaped a couple of plates with food, and asked me to take them up to Cousin Sophy's room.

"For such frail creatures they eat more than a field hand," she grumbled as she slapped the plates on a tray. "And why they have to be served in their room beats me. If she weren't paying me extry, believe you me, they'd be sitting up to the table same as everyone else."

As I passed through the hall, one of the lawmen was nailing something to the wall. I didn't notice what it was, for my attention was drawn to a giggling voice.

"Oh, Jakey, you are just too-too clever. Parsing* that sentence like that."

Sure enough, Lilybell was enthroned on the top step with her flouncy skirt spread out and her schoolwork sitting on her lap. She gazed up at Jake as he hung over the stair railing spellbound. *Those blue eyes are enough to charm a hermit,* I thought glumly.

I longed to box Jake's ears and kick Lilybell down the steps. God couldn't have meant Lilybell when He'd said, "Charity envieth not." I overcame my desire to kick her and kicked the trunk instead.

After knocking on Cousin Sophy's door, I again felt a cold draft from under it and thought I heard the outside door close. After she let me in, I smelled cigar smoke in the room. Could Cousin Sophy have had a whiskey customer? It seemed likely.

She instructed me to set the tray on the trunk. So I did, then giving in to an impulse, gave the trunk a good swift kick. The results were a hollow-sounding thud and a sore toe.

Cousin Sophy's eyebrows shot up, but she didn't say a word, as I made a hasty exit, running into Lilybell as she minced into the room.

Jake was still hanging around the top of the stairs. I intended to pass him without speaking, but he acted just as though Lilybell hadn't come between us.

"Susie, did you see what that government investigator tacked to the wall?"

"No, what?" I asked, forgetting all about being aloof.

"A 'wanted' poster. Come on down and let's look at it."

Underneath the picture of a man smiling with a cigar in his mouth were the words:

Henry Standard

WANTED

for Promoting and Selling

Dishonest Stock in the

"Gold Bug Mine"

Located in Dry Gulch, Oregon

Jake leaned over, his hair tickling my ear, and whispered, "Pa says the investigators are sure he's somewhere around here. They had his cabin in Dry Gulch surrounded, then he vanished into thin air. But they think he's headed this way."

"Honest!" I exclaimed as I stepped back and studied the picture. "Something about the smile does look familiar."

"I've never seen him, but we need to be on the lookout. It'd be a feather in Pa's cap if he could catch him."

Suddenly, I remembered my current feeling regarding Jake and said, "I'm sure darling Lilybell will be delighted to assist you. I've enough to do, figuring out what her mother is doing with a trunk load of whiskey."

I whirled around and started toward the kitchen.

Jake stepped in front of me. "Susie, what are you rattling on about?"

"Nothing you'd be interested in, at the moment, anyway. Now kindly step aside."

5
Problems with a Periscope

Saturday sped by with Mrs. Higgins barking out orders. For a start, I had to change the lawmen's beds, since they had left town.

Then she wanted the rest of the hotel dust completely rearranged. So with mopping, dusting, and washing, I barely had time to catch my breath—let alone get another glimpse of the trunk.

Once on my way to the kitchen with an armload of dirty bedding, I caught Lilybell studying the "wanted" poster.

"That smile sure looks familiar," I told her.

"I doubt it," she contradicted.

"Take that cigar out of his mouth, and the mouth and chin remind me of someone I've seen. Hmmmmm."

"It's only your imagination," she insisted as she stamped her little foot and changed the subject. "This drafty old hotel is so tiresome today." (Jake worked at *The Chronicle* on Saturdays.)

"Idle hands are the devil's workshop," I quoted, ignoring the fact that God said, "Charity . . . is kind."

Tommy spent the day constructing a periscope to use for spying on Cousin Sophy. Sarah had loaned us a couple of small mirrors the night before. She told us she'd skin us alive if we didn't return them in one piece. Neither of us took her too seriously. Love had done wonders for her disposition.

Since the parsonage was in its usual Saturday night uproar, Tommy and I didn't have any trouble getting permission to dash over to the hotel for a few minutes.

For my part, I'd just as soon stayed home and continued my investigation of the trunk at a later date. I didn't have any more zip than a wet mop. Even the Saturday night bustle failed to stir me up.

Mama and Sarah pressed and sponged Sunday clothes, while Aunt Minnie charged around supervising the heating of bath water.

Joe's screeching "Murder!" when Aunt Minnie scoured his ears blended with Papa's preaching voice. Papa followed Mama around like a puppy, practicing tomorrow's sermon from the "Love Chapter."

And I had the strongest desire to sit down with my feet on the oven door. But Tommy'd worked hard on his periscope and I knew I couldn't disappoint him.

"Charity . . . seeketh not her own," I reminded myself as I wrapped a scarf around my head and followed Tommy out the back door.

The night was clear, with all the stars twinkling like jewels, while the moon lent a friendly light. The cold caused the pipe to stick to Tommy's mittens and chased away my weariness.

"It's light enough; we'll be able to see the steps," I commented.

"Yeah, I figured we'd better not bother with a lantern, so I'm glad it's so clear out."

After we crept to the top of the stairs, Tommy adjusted the mirrors. Then he held the pipe up so one end faced the window over the door. He peered into the other end.

"Can't see a thing," he muttered as he lowered the pipe and moved the mirrors about. He worked without making a sound.

I shook my hands and softly shook my feet to keep them from freezing.

Tommy raised the pipe again. "It's working," he whispered excitedly. "But all I can see is the wallpaper."

"I-I-I'm freezing, Tommy. H-hurry up."

"I'll just have to set this top mirror, so it slopes down more," he told me as he stuck his mittened hand into the top of the pipe.

Then it happened! With a little clunk, the mirror fell, hitting the railing of the platform where we were, and dropping to the snow-covered ground below.

"Tommy, we've got to go down and find that mirror! Remember what Sarah said about wanting it back."

"Rats, you're—" Tommy stopped and shoved me into the far corner of the platform, just as the door opened.

Cousin Sophy stuck her head out the door and looked down the steps.

"There doesn't seem to be anyone out here, Lilybell. I thought I heard him coming back," she called over her shoulder, as she shut the door.

"Let's get out of here," Tommy blurted out.

We hustled down the steps as fast as the moonlight and the kitchen plumbing allowed.

Neither of us said anything, but my curiosity felt overloaded. *Who did they expect back? Could it be Jake? But why would he call by the back door when he lived right down the hall? They must be expecting a whiskey customer,* I decided.

Tommy interrupted my thoughts with, "Now we've got to find that mirror. In about three feet of snow, we'll have some fun doing it, but maybe it won't be broken."

We made our way toward the back of the hotel.

Just as we rounded the corner of the steps, we saw a man leaning against the wall smoking a cigar. He was looking away from us, so we were right next to him before he realized we were there.

He glanced around, gave a grunt, then took off like a pistol shot.

"Who was that?" I asked, after he'd disappeared from sight.

"Beats me, but maybe it was a boarder on his way to the little house out back*."

"I know all the boarders, unless a new one moved in tonight. Besides, he didn't need to tear off like that, unless he's up to no good."

"We'll be no good if we don't find Sarah's mirror," Tommy reminded me, as he crouched down and peered over the snow below the porch platform.

He'd been looking only a minute, when he yelled,

"I've found it and it's not broken or anything!"

As we set out for home, my cold feet felt dead, but my mind was a-buzzing.

"Everything points to that trunk being full of whiskey," I told Tommy.

"Not necessarily."

"That man must have been a whiskey customer."

"Susie, two whiskey bottles sitting on a trunk doesn't mean there's a trunk full of them. Maybe the bottles didn't even have whiskey in them. And how does that figure in with something in that trunk moving?"

"Don't forget the footprints, cigar-smoke smell, and the outside door opening every time I knock on the hall one," I stubbornly reminded him.

"We'll never find out what's going on till we spy on Cousin Sophy's room with this periscope. I'll work on perfecting it," Tommy promised as we hurried toward the warm lights of home.

6
A Wrong Guess

The cold snap lasted through Sunday. Everyone from the parsonage but Abby and Timmy shivered across the yard to the church. Only a handful of townspeople joined us. That Arctic blast forced the ranchers to keep their horses home in warm stables.

Cousin Sophy didn't brave the weather, but Lilybell blew in, clutching Jake's arm. The wind had whipped a rosy color into her pearly cheeks. It was no wonder Jake couldn't stop gazing at her.

I figured my cheeks were green, with envy, that is. Papa's preaching from the "Love Chapter" gave me an uncomfortable feeling somewhere close to the heart. When he got to the part that says "charity envieth not," the feeling became a downright pain. If this was lovesickness, I hoped I'd soon recover.

The day didn't improve.

Mama felt Joe's forehead as he stumbled through the kitchen door after church.

"Oh, dear, you're burning with fever. Right to bed you go," she ordered, while the little creases between her eyes deepened.

Then, Tommy not wanting any supper caused Mama to hustle him off to bed.

The ones of us still able to sit at the table were picking at our food, when Sidney brought Sarah home from spending the afternoon with his family.

After Sidney left and Sarah learned that two more of us had fallen victim to the influenza, she decided to postpone her wedding.

"Oh, dear, I do dislike you postponing your wedding," Mama sighed, after Sarah had shared her thoughts with us. "After all, Sidney's parents are only waiting till the wedding next Saturday, before taking the stage to Sidney's grandmother's. You know they don't expect her to live much longer and Mrs. Wright does want to see her as soon as possible."

"And," Mama continued, "the rooms over the

drugstore are all ready for you to live in and the word is out that the wedding will be next Saturday. Of course, with all the sickness and bad weather we can't expect too many, but still—"

"Sure and Sidney'll be ruining his stomach baching," Aunt Minnie insisted. "And it's no one that will be knowing, but what the weather'll improve by Saturday next."

"That's true," Sarah agreed, "but, who'll take care of all the sick ones? I won't have a wedding without Papa to marry me and Mama and Aunt Minnie to be witnesses. And I've always had my heart set on Abby playing the organ."

"Still and all, I'm for thinking we'd best carry on with the wedding," Papa told Sarah as he ran his big hands through his hair.

"Maybe Mrs. Miller could play the organ and I'll stay home and play nurse," Abby suggested, her freckles standing out on her long, pale face. Her disappointment was showing.

Abby'd never been pretty, like Sarah, but she was so good-natured that it seldom crossed a person's mind. With her so peaked-looking and shaky from her sickness, I knew I couldn't stand by and keep her from Sarah's wedding.

"I'll stay home and take care of the sick ones," I blurted out, before I had time to remind myself of how I'd been looking forward to being in on the first wedding in the family.

Papa beamed at me. "Susie, it'll be you that's remembering love seeketh not her own."

"Thank you, Susie," Sarah whispered, as she reached across the table and squeezed my hand. If I'd been a cat, I would have purred.

Aunt Minnie's bedchamber was turned into a sick room for the three boys. Mama spent all Sunday night in there bathing their foreheads in an attempt to break the fevers.

But, when I looked in before leaving for school Monday, Tommy's was still high. He was mumbling about the periscope. "Get the periscope, Susie, the periscope."

Mama and Aunt Minnie, scurrying between the beds, didn't pay any attention to his mutterings. But I did. It was up to me to carry out his wishes. After all, I was the one who'd started him on this investigation in the first place.

With the hubbub of nursing three sick boys, slipping out of the house with the periscope that evening was simple.

The night air felt balmy compared to yesterday's. I marched straight over to the hotel, up the outside steps, and to my cousin's door.

I held the periscope up to the window just like

Tommy'd done on Saturday night. I couldn't see a thing, but thought I heard a man's voice. Could it be another whiskey customer?

There were no two ways about it, I had to have a look inside that trunk. I feverishly refitted the mirrors, then held the long pipe up to the window again. This time the mirrors reflected the floor. As I moved the pipe around, the trunk came into view. And it was wide open! The lid lay back against the wall revealing the entire inside!

This threw me into such a dither, I nearly whooped with joy. But I caught myself in time and stared at the trunk, like an eagle after a field mouse.

I might as well have stayed home for all I learned. I found out the trunk was lined with a flowery paper and that there was something dark in the very bottom.

However, the light from their lamp left the bottom of the trunk in shadows. My spying did reveal one thing. I was a poor guesser. The trunk wasn't full of whiskey bottles.

Although I did everything but stand on my head, I couldn't find another clue as to the odd happenings surrounding that trunk.

Just then, I heard someone push the bolt back from the lock on the other side of the door.

I took off down those steps as if a timber wolf

were after me. I'd have gotten away with no one
the wiser too, but the warmer weather had made the
steps as slick as glass.

Three steps from the bottom, my left foot slid off
into space. My right foot promptly followed and in
a twinkling I slid to the foot of the stairs, landing
in the snow.

There I lay, sprawled out but still clutching the
pipe, when Jake came whistling out of Lilybell's
door.

"Susie, is that you?" he exclaimed as he de-
scended and the light of his lantern fell on my face.
"What happened? Are you hurt? Here, let me help
you up."

"I'm all right, Jake," I mumbled, as I gave him
my hand and he pulled me to my feet.

"Susie, what in creation is that thing you're hold-
ing? It looks like a pipe. What's going on anyway?"

I'd never been so flustered in my life. A lady just
doesn't tell the "object of her affections" that she's
been spying on someone with the kitchen plumbing.
Any admiration he might feel for her would plunge
to nothing.

"I need to get home in a hurry," I told a
bewildered-looking Jake. And I took off for home
at full speed.

7
A Ruined Chance

Tuesday morning, Tommy was still tossing around in bed, but Sis was able to totter into school.

I nearly knocked her over with a bear hug.

"Susie!" she shrieked.

"Am I glad to see you. I've sure missed you!"

"Quick, tell me everything that's happened since I've been laid low."

"Remember Lilybell? And her mother's huge trunk? The heavy one she acted so secretive about? Well, since I heard the strange noises in it, I've seen whiskey bottles on it and smelled cigar smoke in the room. And . . ."

I caught my breath and whispered, "Tommy and I even tried spying on them with an invention of his, but I'll have to admit, I haven't the foggiest notion of what's in that trunk."

Sis brushed the mystery of the trunk away with a wave of her hand. "Oh, phooey on that trunk, Susie. What I want to know is, how's the romance coming?"

"Ah, well, um," my sputtering was cut short by Miss Prim ringing the school bell. Some things are too "close to the heart" to share with even a best friend.

The next day, being Valentine's Day, Miss Prim permitted us to put our books away early. That's when the fun began

I passed out the heart-shaped cookies Aunt Minnie had baked for me to share with my classmates. Then Miss Prim instructed Jake to deliver any valentine greetings from the "Valentine Post Office Box."

Jake flashed me a big grin when he flipped a store-bought card on my desk. It said:

> The rose is red, the violet blue ·
> Sugar is sweet, and so are you.
> If you love me, as I love you,
> No knife can cut our love in two.

The card was clever with its roses and violets and a knife hitting a big heart, but failing to cut it in two.

I figured it was from Sis, as we are special friends. I smiled a "thank-you" to her across the room.

After Jake had delivered most of the valentines to the proper desks, he sheepishly pulled a large one out of the box. It was addressed to him in a flowery handwriting. It reeked of perfume and had enough ruffles on it to trim a dress.

By the smirk on Lilybell's face, I knew she'd given it to him and judging by the titters from the boys, they knew too. Jake, turning as red as the paper heart he held, slipped it under a book on his desk.

My hearts and cupids mood vanished. I barely managed to thank my friends for the sweet little verses they'd penned on their cards to me.

And since Sis had to stay after school to make up the studies she'd missed while being sick, I didn't get a chance to thank her for the "knife" valentine or the homemade one she'd given me.

I hurried off to the hotel, where Mrs. Higgins met me at the door with a mile-long list of jobs to be done.

Peeling potatoes and stoking wood into the stove,

while listening to Mrs. Higgins ramble on, momentarily kept my mind from the pains brought on by lovesickness.

The crushing blow came when Mrs. Higgins sent me up to Cousin Sophy's room with their tray.

Lilybell, who seemed to be alone, opened the door with a gleaming smile on her face.

"Good evening, Susie. Set the tray on the table."

I followed her directions and nearly set the tray on that satin-covered candy box that Sis and I had admired in the window of Wright's Drugstore.

It was even more magnificent upon close scrutiny. A huge, red bow rested on the puffed-up, red satin that covered the heart-shaped box.

And the chocolaty smell that escaped when Lilybell lifted the lid nearly bowled me over.

"Would you care for a candy?" she asked sweetly. "An admirer of mine gave them to me."

"No, thank you," I choked out. I was positive Jake's love-gift to Lilybell would strangle me.

"They're really yummy," she told me as she popped one in her mouth.

I whirled around, almost rammed into the trunk, then fled.

When I reached the top of the stairs, I stopped, unclenched my fists, and took a deep breath.

Then it hit me. I'd nearly fallen over the wide-

open trunk and hadn't even glanced into it!!

Forgetting that "charity envieth not" had ruined my big moment.

8
Look-
Alikes

By Thursday, wedding preparations were going forward at breakneck speed.

Mama stayed up late gathering a taffeta petticoat to go under Sarah's wedding dress. And somehow, between her other work she squeezed in time to take up the seams on Abby's best dress. Abby drooped about the house now, but she'd never gain her normal weight back before the wedding.

Aunt Minnie chopped off the heads of all the chickens that had given up egg laying. These were cooked up to go in a chicken salad for the wedding reception. Sarah'd read where chicken salad was served at all the "best" wedding receptions back East.

The invalids improved along with the weather, but Mama wouldn't let any of them out of the house for fear of a relapse.

Tommy recovered enough to ask about the periscope. "Did you ever get it to work, Susie?"

"Yeah," I told him while I perched on the edge of his bed. "I even looked into the trunk. But I couldn't tell much from those little-bitty mirrors, so I gave them back to Sarah. She's trying a new hairstyle for her wedding and needs them to see the back of her head."

"You didn't see any whiskey bottles in the trunk, did you?" he asked me as he propped his head up with the palm of his hand.

"No, guess Cousin Sophy isn't a bootlegger after all. It seemed like such a good idea, considering the bottles on the trunk, the cigar smoke, and her needing that outside door. Then, finding those man-sized footprints on the steps and seeing that sneaky-acting cigar smoker pointed straight at bootlegging."

"It didn't figure in with your hearing something move in the trunk, though," Tommy reminded me.

"Sure is a puzzle. Makes a person as curious as a cat, as to what Jake and Papa carried up to her room in that trunk. It was lots heavier than clothes. I ought to know, I helped shove."

"Maybe we'll never find out," Tommy sighed and flopped back on his pillow.

"I mean to; I'm not giving up. I'll just keep my mind off other things and never let another chance pass without looking into that trunk."

The next evening after school, I hustled over to the hotel. Mama had instructed me to help Mrs. Higgins all I could. She'd offered us the use of the hotel dining room for the wedding reception the next day.

I was briskly whisking the broom around chair legs, when Jake ambled into the dining room.

He grabbed the broom and gave me his big grin. "You look dangerous with that thing, Susie."

I made a face at him and ordered, "Give that back. I've got to get this place cleaned up for the wedding reception."

I wasn't about to give him a chance to inquire about Monday night's affair with the pipe.

"The wedding's what I need to talk with you about, Susie. Pa is getting ready to leave right now. There's a new lead on 'Old Smiley' from the 'wanted' poster out in the hall."

"Really," I exclaimed as we went into the hall to get another look at Henry Standard. He smiled down from his picture, just as though he'd never done a dishonest deed in his life.

"Yeah, Pa's bound and determined he's going to get him. Show all the big law officers that a little-town sheriff can catch a wanted man, after they let him slip through their fingers."

"I hope he does, Jake, but what's that got to do with Sarah's wedding?"

"Well, Pa thinks there should be a big write-up in the paper and he doesn't have the time to do it. Since they do own the only drugstore in Horseshoe Bend, the Wrights are pretty important people. And so is the preacher's family. So, Pa's assigning the job to me. I thought," and Jake looked down at his hands and popped a couple of knuckles. "I thought, maybe you'd sit with me during the wedding and help me. Girls are better at telling about dresses and such."

"Oh, Jake, I'd like to! But I can't. I told my family I'd stay with the boys. They're still pretty sick. Of course, Abby did say she would, but I couldn't be so mean-hearted. She's more Sarah's age and Sarah has her heart set on Abby playing the organ. Maybe—"

"Good evening," Lilybell interrupted. She'd tip-toed up behind us, her skirts rustling and her creamy cheeks dimpling.

"Hello," I answered, while Jake stared at the floor, not saying a word.

"Ooh, you'll not believe the simply heavenly dress I'm wearing to the wedding tomorrow. It's just so special, but I'll not whisper another word about it. I want it to be a surprise. And Jakey, you'll be seeing me over to the church, won't you? I'd just die if I slipped in this slushy snow and dirtied my dress."

She gave Jake her most gorgeous smile, but he continued staring at the floor and murmured, "Ummmmmmm."

Then he looked up and said, "I've got to get upstairs, so Pa can give me some last-minute directions."

He left us, taking the steps two at a time.

Jake disappeared so rapidly that Lilybell was still wearing her special "Jakey smile" when she turned toward me.

I nearly fainted! Her smile (minus the cigar) matched the smile of Henry Standard on the "wanted" poster. I stared at the man on the poster, then turned to compare his smile to Lilybell's.

But Lilybell was gone. She'd slipped away without a rustle.

"Now, what can all that mean?" I asked myself as I continued to chase dust balls across the floor.

9
What the Trunk Held

The morning of the wedding, I staggered down-stairs, rubbing sleep from my eyes. I found Mama and Aunt Minnie, who'd been up since before dawn, whizzing around the kitchen.

Mama had the fire in the stove crackling and popping in order to get the sadirons* spitting-hot. She carefully pushed them over the pressing cloth covering the wedding dress, while the yards and yards of white taffeta billowed around her feet.

Aunt Minnie made little peaks in the boiled icing she'd spread over the tall wedding cake.

"And the top of the morning to you," she greeted

73

me, as she stood back to survey her handiwork on that three-tiered cake. "And if 'tis breakfast you be wanting, you'd best serve yourself. Mush is on the back of the stove."

Mama looked up from her work. "Susie, before you eat, would you please step into my bedchamber and bring Abby's dress to me? I'll need to press those seams I took in."

I nearly blurted out, "Why can't Abby stay home, so I can go to the wedding? After all, it's not every day I'm invited to sit by Horseshoe Bend's most handsome young man."

But before I had time to give words to my selfish thoughts, I noticed once again those new lines (maybe they'd always been there) between Mama's eyes. Then I looked at Aunt Minnie stooping over the cake and remembered all the hours she'd spent making the fixings for the wedding reception. Beautiful Lilybell could snuggle up to Jake to her heart's content, before I'd let on to my family how much I wanted to go to the wedding.

"Happy the bride, the sun shines on," Aunt Minnie told us later, after the sun arose in a clear blue sky.

The nine of us stopped eating our mush and stared at the kitchen window where the sun blazed through the panes.

Papa began singing, "Praise God from whom all blessings flow." The rest of us joyfully joined in, although Joe said it hurt his throat to sing.

From then on until the wedding in the afternoon, the house was in a happy jumble.

"Sure and where'd my shaving mug get to?"

"I don't need no more of that nasty tasting stuff. I'm well, honest."

"Mama, I need you to fasten my petticoat."

"Here comes Grandpa Murdock to carry the wedding cake over to the hotel."

"Susie, you be the one to give the lemonade a taste."

"Lookee, lookee, what Sidney sent over! Flowers for the bride."

"Stand back so I can see if that veil is draping properly."

We were all struck speechless as we gathered around Sarah in her bridal finery.

Her dress looked like a Paris fashion plate. Mama had made it with a high lace neck and frilly jabot*. The broad leg-of-mutton sleeves* accented her thin-as-a-wasp's waist.

Whenever she so much as breathed, the billowing skirts rustled. I just knew Sidney's heart would turn over when he claimed Sarah for his bride.

Aunt Minnie broke the silence with a deep sigh.

Then she said, "Sure and you're looking like an angel."

Joe, who'd tired of gazing at Sarah, yelled, "There's the Coopers from clear over by Birdsong Creek, turning in the churchyard."

"Mercy, is it that late already!" someone gasped, and everyone scattered.

Tommy and I positioned ourselves by the kitchen window so we could watch people arriving at the church for the wedding.

Tommy, wrapped up in a quilt, and I in my best dress (for I was attending the reception, while Abby played nurse) discussed the activity in front of the church.

"There's Sis Miller," I told Tommy as I tapped on the window to get her attention.

"And, there's Cousin Sophy and Lilybell. And we still don't know what they're up to," Tommy commented. Then he asked, "Where's Jake?"

"I wouldn't know. Tommy, did you know that Lilybell's smile looks just like the man's smile on the 'wanted' poster?"

"Hmmmm."

"Say, Tommy, this would be a perfect time to look in their trunk."

"It might be locked."

"But it might not be. Just think everyone from

the hotel is over at the church. If only I hadn't promised Mama I'd stay here with you boys."

"I'm not that sick, Susie; if you really want to go over to the hotel, go ahead."

"But what if one of you needed something? Mama'd be awfully upset if any of you went outside of the house."

"This might be your only chance, though, Susie. Wowee, look at that crowd! This good weather's really bringing them out of the woodwork," Tommy finished wistfully.

Then I knew that Tommy felt as badly as I did about missing all the doings. Even if I never found out the trunk's secret, I couldn't go off and leave him alone with Timmy and Joe.

Tommy interrupted my thoughts with, "There's Jake waving at us."

Jake seemed to be the last wedding guest, so Tommy and I left our place by the window. A churchyard full of sleighs and blanketed horses didn't much interest us.

Before the little boys had time to wake up, Abby stumbled in the back door.

"What's wrong, Abby?" I asked as I helped her to the rocker by the stove.

She fell into the chair before answering. "I'm just terribly weak is all, Susie. How about a cup of tea? I made it fine through the wedding, but it's a good thing I didn't plan on the reception."

By the time I'd gotten Abby her tea and headed for the hotel, all the wedding guests were crowded into the hotel dining room.

I noticed as soon as I opened the hotel door that a noise like a flock of birds on a spring morning poured from the dining room.

The hall seemed lonely in comparison. I glanced up the stairs. Upstairs seemed deserted too. Everyone in Horseshoe Bend was busy either congratulating the happy pair, guzzling lemonade, or just plain enjoying each other's company.

Everyone meant Cousin Sophy and Lilybell too. And that meant they weren't in their room.

I zipped up the stairs.

A stab of guilt pricked me when I wrapped my fingers around the doorknob. But I ignored it. I'd waited too long for this chance.

The window shades were up and the late afternoon sunlight slanting in the window gleamed on the big brass key stuck in the brass lock.

I tiptoed over to the trunk, turned the key, and lifted the lid.

Outside of a dark-blue quilt folded on the bottom, the trunk looked empty.

I leaned over to look under the quilt when the

outside door opened. I shot up and whirled around in time to see a man coming through the door.

"What're you doing here?" I demanded.

"I might ask you the same thing," he said as he pushed the door shut behind him.

"This happens to be my cousin's room," I informed him.

"This happens to be my wife's room."

"Cousin Sophy is a widow, I'll have you to know."

"My, aren't we the sassy one," he answered. Then he asked, "What makes you say she's a widow?"

"She said so herself and she wears black widow's clothes."

"That don't make her a widow, though," he informed me as he sat down and pulled a cigar from his shirt pocket.

"Cigars! Have you been in this room before?"

"I've been living here for about a week."

"Oh! Now I see—why the lock on the door, needing an outside door, and the extra food on the tray. And, and the man's footprints in the snow, the drafts from that outside door, and the cigar smoke. And the whiskey bottles! You do drink whiskey, don't you?"

"What are you, a member of the Prohibition Party*?" he asked me with a smirky smile.

Why, his smile looks just like Lilybell's, I thought

to myself. Then it hit me! Lilybell's smile looked like the man's on the "wanted" poster.

"Say, you're the crook from the 'wanted' poster," I told him.

"My, you are clever, but not very polite, calling me a crook."

"You vanished from sight when the law officers had your cabin surrounded, then here you show up in the Grande Hotel. How'd you get here without them seeing you?"

"Blew in during a storm," he told me as he glanced behind me.

I turned around to see where he was looking. The trunk! He'd escaped from Dry Gulch hidden in the trunk.

His lighting a match on the sole of his shoe jarred me to my senses. I let out a squeal and tore out of the room and down the stairs.

I stopped with a thump, when I plowed into Sheriff Evans' belt buckle.

"Sheriff, he's up there, Cousin Sophy's husband," I squeaked out. "The man from the 'wanted' poster."

"The who?"

"The crook! Henry Standard or Stoddard or whatever his name is."

"Great thunderations! And here I've been gallivanting all over the country and he's right under my nose," he sputtered as he leaped up the stairs three at a time.

Then I thought of the back door through which Cousin Sophy's husband could easily escape.

I ran into the dining room and called out, "Sheriff Evans needs some help catching that crook."

It seemed like a thousand pairs of eyes turned to look at me in the doorway.

"And what shenanigans be you up to, Susie?" Papa boomed out in the now silent room.

"The crook's about to escape down the back stairs," I told him.

Papa didn't stop to ask any more questions, but grabbed Jake and tore out of the room.

The wedding guests rushed out of the dining room like water from a sieve. The bride and groom were forgotten as the crowd pushed out the door and spilled onto the hotel porch.

Cousin Sophy, pulling Lilybell behind her, shoved her way through the guests, muttering, "Someone's discovered Henry."

I'd made it to the porch railing, when Sheriff Evans snapped the handcuffs on Cousin Sophy's husband.

With her chin jutting out, she held onto his arm, and told everyone assembled there, "My husband isn't going to jail without Lilybell and me."

"If this doesn't beat all!" Sheriff Evans declared. "While I've been scouring the countryside for him, he's been living under the same roof with me. Guess I shouldn't feel too bad, though. He slipped by those big government law officers when they had his cabin surrounded."

"Now, how'd you manage that, I'd like to know?" he asked the still cigar-smoking Henry What's-His-Name.

Cousin Sophy's husband smiled and nodded his head at me. "Ask that redheaded busybody—she can tell you."

I know my face matched my hair, as once again all those pairs of eyes looked my way. "The trunk," I murmured, just as Mama slipped her arm around me.

"The government lawmen even helped me load the trunk on the sleigh at Dry Gulch," Cousin Sophy informed us. "People are always willing to help a widow."

" 'Tis past believing, but Jake and I hefted that trunk into their room. Faith, and it were heavy." Papa chuckled at the memory.

A festive mood settled on everyone once again and they all trooped inside to finish their cake.

"I'll be locking him up for the night," the sheriff told the few of us left on the porch. "We'll be

shipping him up to a bigger jail for the government law officers to take care of tomorrow."

"Lilybell and I'll be coming along too," Cousin Sophy repeated. She looked as though it would take more than the law to separate her from her husband.

"I imagine it would do no good to invite her to the house to stay," Mama decided.

"Mama, how come she's sticking by that hooligan? After all he's done."

"I expect because she loves him, Susie."

"Loves him, how could she? What'll she get out of sticking with a crook?"

"Loving is giving, not getting," Mama reminded me. "Jesus was our very best Example. Think of what He gave up, His very life, for our wretched ones. And I would think that after today, I wouldn't have to remind you that love seeketh not her own."

Mama stopped, gave me a big hug, then continued, "Who was it that gave up her big wish of attending the wedding, so those she loved could be there?"

I hugged Mama back, then told her, "I'm apt to miss the reception too. I *have* to go home and tell Tommy what thumped in the trunk and that the mystery of the giant trunk is solved."

10
Putting Things to Rights

Later that evening Aunt Minnie and I toted buckets and mops over to the hotel. We meant to put the dining room to rights. The wedding reception had left it pretty much in shambles.

Mrs. Higgins met us at the door, with her arms folded across her big front. "Land-to-goodness, that were a lovely wedding."

"Sure and I'm agreeing with that," Aunt Minnie said as she dropped her mop bucket.

"Believe you me, I doubt I'll ever live down harboring a criminal under my roof, though," she declared. "It gives the place a bad name. Susie, get that trashy 'wanted' poster off the wall. I don't favor having that lawbreaker grinning at me."

She and Aunt Minnie went into the dining room muttering about the goings-on, while I carried out her orders.

Jake came down the stairs while I was tearing the poster off the wall.

"Susie, you're just the person I want to see."

"Really?"

"Yeah, how'd you know Henry Standard or Stoddard was in the trunk? I'd never have figured that out. Even Pa's impressed, though he's too ashamed to admit it."

"Well, to make a long story short, I'd have to say that he the same as told me. Not that I didn't try to find out about that trunk, but I spent most of my time barking up the wrong tree."

"I think you did real good, Susie."

Mrs. Higgins stuck her head around the door, and seeing that I'd finished the job she'd given me, said, "You two scoot up to the Stoddard's room and bring that big trunk down here.

"When she came back for her things, she told me she'd never set foot in this place again. Just as though we were the dishonest ones. Humph," Mrs. Higgins sniffed. "Anyways, that trunk will make a mighty good place to store the blankets off the hotel beds. Think spring is coming sometime."

As soon as we entered the room, I noticed that they'd left that satiny, red candy box behind.

"I see Lilybell left your valentine candy box here."

"My candy box!" Jake shouted. "I don't know anything about that candy box."

Then, he lowered his voice, gazed right into my eyes, and told me, "I only bought one valentine."

"Did it have a knife on it?"

"Yeah."

"Thank you, Jake."

"So, this is the mysterious trunk," Jake said, quickly changing the subject.

"I feel sort of sorry for Lilybell having a crook for a father," I told Jake as we looked into its vast interior.

"Yeah."

"Suppose you'll really miss her. She's awfully pretty."

"Yeah, but a guy gets tired of someone using him all the time. If I wasn't doing her schoolwork, I was being her crutch," Jake said as he banged the lid shut. "Come on, Susie, grab the other end."

I did as I was told, then smiled across the length of the trunk at Jake.

He grinned back. "Guess we won't have anyone giving us directions every step of the way, like we did when we strained our muscles carrying that crook up here."

"And to think, a preacher and a sheriff's son did it."

"With the help of a preacher's daughter. A pretty nice preacher's daughter, at that," Jake added as we bumped down the steps.

Life in 1898

HORSESHOE BEND: You'll not find Horseshoe Bend on an Oregon map. But it is patterned after any number of small towns in the high desert country of northeastern Oregon.

INFLUENZA: Influenza is a sickness that today we call "flu." The victims suffer from chills, fevers, headaches, joint aches, and a general weakness. It is spread from person to person by a virus. The epidemics most often occur in winter, because people are in closer contact with one another at this time. The very young, very old, or very weak often died from the complications of influenza before the development of antibiotics and other drugs. Even though we have vaccines today, we often suffer from the same symptoms as the influenza patients in Horseshoe Bend.

IRISH: Since Susie's papa (children seldom called their fathers "Daddy" then) and Aunt Minnie were

Irish, it showed up in their speech and conduct. Most of the Conroys seemed to have inherited their redheaded appearance and exuberant personalities from that side of the family.

LEG-OF-MUTTON SLEEVES: These sleeves were called "leg-of-mutton" because they resembled a ready-to-cook leg of lamb (mutton). Dresses with these sleeves were fashionable when Susie's sister, Sarah, married Sidney. They were made of a large balloon of material at the top of a long, tight sleeve. Between the sleeves, hung the *JABOT*. The "jabot" was made of layers of lace that were attached to the neckline and extended to the snug waist. Below the waist billowing yards of fabric were supported by rustling petticoats. As Lilybell could have told you, braid and ruffle trims put your dress in the "too-too" class. And Cousin Sophy found the custom of wearing *WIDOW'S CLOTHES* to her advantage. Ladies (and some men), in the 1800s, wore black-colored clothing as a sign that they were mourning the death of a loved one.

LOVE: People became as confused about love in 1898 as they do today. Too bad more people don't discover, as Susie did, that real love, God's kind of love, directs itself toward giving—not getting.

MERCANTILE STORE: In Horseshoe Bend, the mercantile store (common name for a "General Store" in the 1800s) sold everything from soda crackers to horse collars.

PARSE: If you'd gone to school with Susie, you'd have used the word "parse" when explaining the form, part of speech, and function of each word in a sentence. Perhaps you've called it "diagraming a sentence." We say "arithmetic" or "math," today, instead of *SUMS.*

PERISCOPE: Tommy explained his periscope quite well. It was a long tube (or drain pipe) with reflecting mirrors on each end, with which he could make observations around corners (or over doors).

SADIRON: In the West, electricity and plumbing were both conveniences of the future. So, instead of plugging an iron into an outlet, the iron was heated on a wood stove. *SAD* means "heavy," and these irons, if used for any length of time, caused pains through the shoulders. No electricity meant houses were lit by *LAMPS* using coal oil or mineral oil kerosene. And the *LITTLE HOUSE OUT BACK* was used in place of bathrooms with indoor plumbing

SALTED MINE: The dictionary describes the process of salting a mine as: artfully depositing minerals in a mine in order to deceive purchasers regarding its value." But, perhaps you like Jake's explanation better. This practice was often carried out during eastern Oregon's 1800 to 1907 mining boom. Shysters, promoting no-good mines, sent flamboyant advertising to people all over the world. This group of wildcat promoters sold stocks in dry holes to millions of innocent investors. As Henry Stoddard found out, the sheriff was often only one step behind. However, we shouldn't forget that there were many honest promoters and stock-brokers selling stocks in proven Oregon mines, also.

TEMPERANCE SOCIETY: In 1898, as today, people were aware of the sadness that excessive drinking of alcohol causes. In the 1800s (and later) many well-meaning people attempted to solve the problem by organizing unions, clubs, or societies to do away with the use of alcohol. A political group, The National *PROHIBITION PARTY,* was founded in 1869, to prevent the sale of liquor or alcoholic beverages in the country. Although these efforts did some good, they failed to change people's desires. For, as Papa believed, only God can do that. With the passage of laws prohibiting the sale of liquor came the *BOOTLEGGERS*. These were people who made, carried, or sold liquor illegally. The practice of concealing illegal objects in the leg of a high boot gave rise to the name "bootlegger."

DO YOU KNOW . . .

what happens when Susie Conroy tries
to ride a bicycle for the first time?

She ends up on the trail of a shifty-
eyed bicycle salesman—and a church
prowler.

Read about her adventures in

The Mystery Man of Horseshoe Bend